# MICKEY'S MYSTERY LIST

Illustrated by the Disney Storybook Artists

© 2014 Disney Enterprises, Inc. All Rights Reserved.

This publication may not be reproduced in whole or in part by any means whatsoever
without written permission from the copyright owners. Permission is never granted for commercial purposes.

Published by Louis Weber, C.E.O., Publications International, Ltd., 7373 North Cicero Avenue, Lincolnwood, Illinois 60712
Ground Floor, 59 Gloucester Place, London W1U 8JJ

Customer Service: 1-800-595-8484 or customer_service@pilbooks.com

**www.pilbooks.com**

p i kids is a registered trademark of Publications International, Ltd.

8 7 6 5 4 3 2 1

Manufactured in China.

ISBN: 978-1-4127-6902-0

publications international, ltd.

It was a perfect day for a surprise party. But first, Minnie needed to go shopping for her surprise party supplies.

So she wrote a shopping list and headed to the store. But a gust of wind blew her list away.

"Oh, dear!" said Minnie. "Whatever will I do now? The surprise party will be ruined without all the surprise party stuff."

Minnie headed back to the Clubhouse, where she told Daisy, Donald, and Goofy the bad news.

"I guess the surprise party is off," she said.

Her friends agreed to look for the lost list.

Outside the Clubhouse, Mickey and Pluto were playing fetch.

"Go get it, boy!" yelled Mickey as he threw a stick to his best friend.

Pluto chased after the stick. But when he returned, he wasn't carrying a stick. He was carrying a piece of paper instead.

"What have you got there, boy?" Mickey asked. "Hm. It says 'Clubhouse Surprise Shopping List.'"

Mickey loved surprises.

"Come on, Pluto," Mickey said. "We'll go shopping for the surprises on this list."

The list was made up of rhyming riddles. Mickey read the first one:

"Pretty to look at,

Pretty to smell,

They'll decorate the party.

It'll be swell!"

Mickey thought about the riddle for a moment. "What look and smell pretty?" he wondered. "I've got it—flowers!"

Mickey hurried to the plant shop, where he bought some beautiful flowers.

Mickey looked at the list again. He read the next riddle:

"The last thing on the list
Came from a seed.
But this next gift
Is something you read."

Mickey thought about this riddle. "What's a gift you can read? Oh, that's an easy one—a book!"

Mickey headed to the bookstore, where he found the perfect gift to read.

Next on the list was a riddle about something with two wheels. Mickey hurried to the bicycle shop, where he found what he needed—a bike!

We've Got Wheels!

The last item was a gift that is worn on the head. "I know what that is," Mickey said. "A hat!" He headed to the hat shop.

Mickey was sure that he'd gotten all of the things on the shopping list. He hurried back to the Clubhouse.

Just as he got back, Mickey noticed that there was one more riddle on the list:

"The last surprise
We'll have to bake
It will be so yummy,
A surprise party ----!"

Mickey was sad that he hadn't had time to bake the last item.

But as Mickey headed inside with his
other surprises, HE was in for a surprise.
"Happy birthday!" the whole gang
shouted, with a cake they had baked
for Mickey!

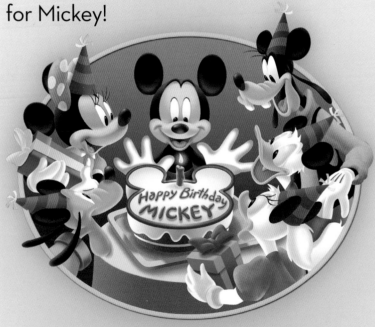